D1074810

GHOSTLY GRAPHIC ADVENTURES

CHASING WHALES ABOARD THE CHARLES W. MORGAN

Written by Baron Specter
Illustrated by Dustin Evans

visit us at www.abdopublishing.com

Published by Magic Wagon, a division of the ABDO Group, 8000 West 78th Street, Edina, Minnesota 55439. Copyright © 2011 by Abdo Consulting Group, Inc. International copyrights reserved in all countries. All rights reserved. No part of this book may be reproduced in any form without written permission from the publisher.

Graphic Planet™ is a trademark and logo of Magic Wagon.

Printed in the United States of America, North Mankato, Minnesota
032010
092010
This book contains at least 10% recycled materials.

Written by Baron Specter
Illustrated by Dustin Evans
Lettered and designed by Ardden Entertainment LLC
Edited by Stephanie Hedlund and Rochelle Baltzer
Cover art by Dustin Evans
Cover design by Ardden Entertainment LLC

Library of Congress Cataloging-in-Publication Data

Specter, Baron, 1957-
   The second adventure : chasing whales aboard the Charles W. Morgan / by Baron Specter ; illustrated by Dustin Evans.
        p. cm. -- (Ghostly graphic adventures)
   Summary: While in Mystic Seaport, Connecticut, Joey and Tank board a whaler that is on display and soon find themselves part of its ghostly crew.
   ISBN 978-1-60270-771-9
  1. Graphic novels. [1. Graphic novels. 2. Ghosts--Fiction. 3. Time travel--Fiction. 4. Whaling--Fiction. 5. Seafaring life--Fiction. 6. Mystic (Conn.)--Fiction.] I. Evans, Dustin, 1982- ill. II. Title. III. Title: Chasing whales aboard the Charles W. Morgan.
   PZ7.7.S648Sec 2010
   741.5'973--dc22
                        2009052722

TABLE OF CONTENTS

OUR HEROES AND VILLAINS

The Cook
Villain

Oarsman
Villain

Joey DeAngelo
Hero

Tank
Hero

Mrs. DeAngelo
Joey's Mom

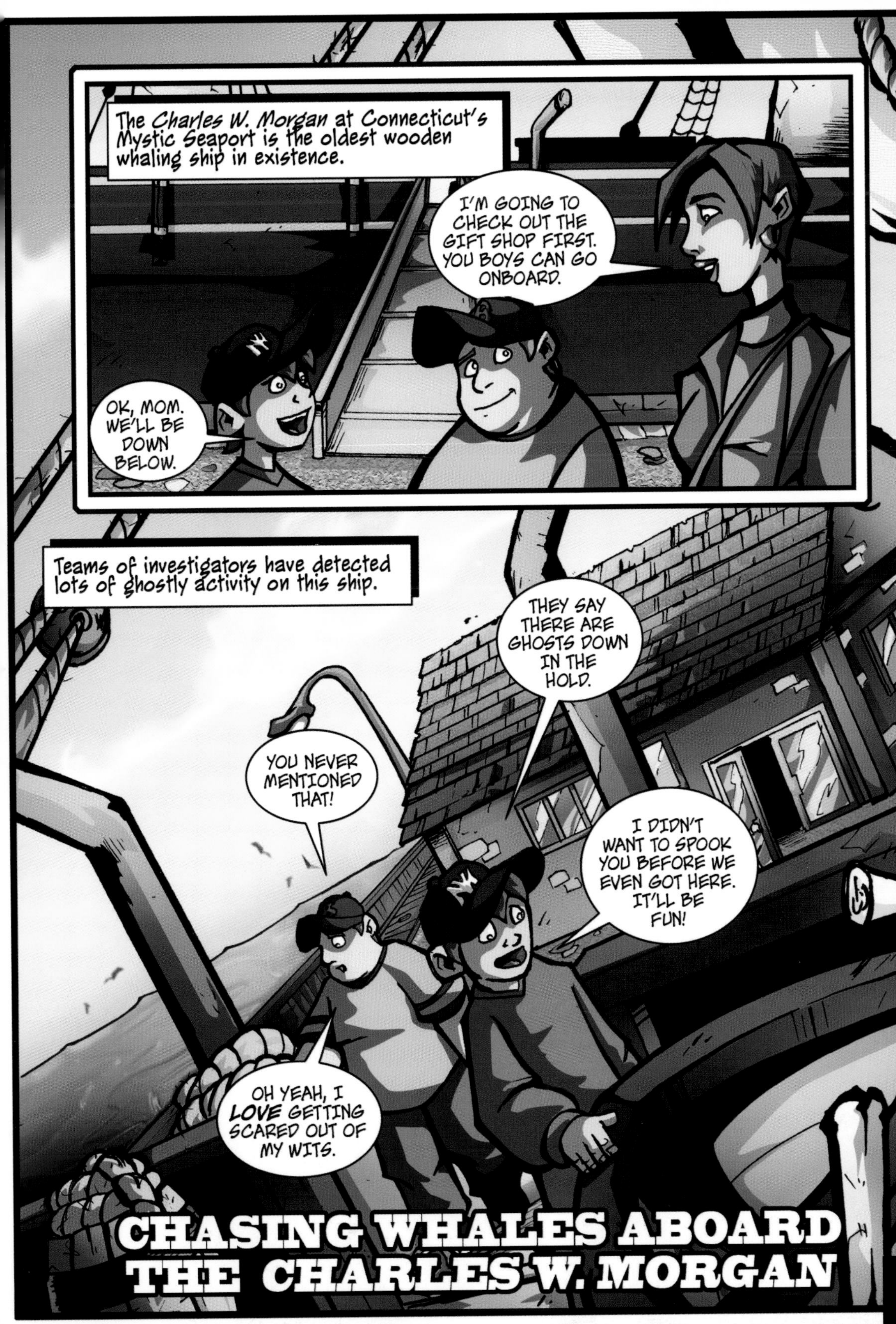

The Charles W. Morgan at Connecticut's Mystic Seaport is the oldest wooden whaling ship in existence.
I'M GOING TO CHECK OUT THE GIFT SHOP FIRST. YOU BOYS CAN GO ONBOARD.
OK, MOM. WE'LL BE DOWN BELOW.
Teams of investigators have detected lots of ghostly activity on this ship.
THEY SAY THERE ARE GHOSTS DOWN IN THE HOLD.
YOU NEVER MENTIONED THAT!
I DIDN'T WANT TO SPOOK YOU BEFORE WE EVEN GOT HERE. IT'LL BE FUN!
OH YEAH, I **LOVE** GETTING SCARED OUT OF MY WITS.
CHASING WHALES ABOARD THE CHARLES W. MORGAN

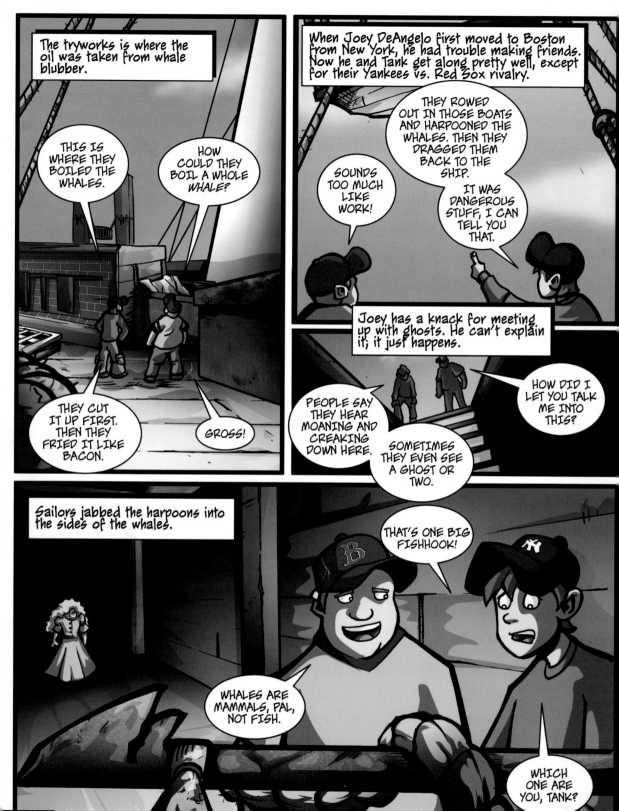

The tryworks is where the oil was taken from whale blubber.

THIS IS WHERE THEY BOILED THE WHALES.

HOW COULD THEY BOIL A WHOLE WHALE?

THEY CUT IT UP FIRST. THEN THEY FRIED IT LIKE BACON.

GROSS!

When Joey DeAngelo first moved to Boston from New York, he had trouble making friends. Now he and Tank get along pretty well, except for their Yankees vs. Red Sox rivalry.

THEY ROWED OUT IN THOSE BOATS AND HARPOONED THE WHALES. THEN THEY DRAGGED THEM BACK TO THE SHIP.

SOUNDS TOO MUCH LIKE WORK!

IT WAS DANGEROUS STUFF, I CAN TELL YOU THAT.

Joey has a knack for meeting up with ghosts. He can't explain it; it just happens.

PEOPLE SAY THEY HEAR MOANING AND CREAKING DOWN HERE.

SOMETIMES THEY EVEN SEE A GHOST OR TWO.

HOW DID I LET YOU TALK ME INTO THIS?

Sailors jabbed the harpoons into the sides of the whales.

THAT'S ONE BIG FISHHOOK!

WHALES ARE MAMMALS, PAL, NOT FISH.

WHICH ONE ARE YOU, TANK?

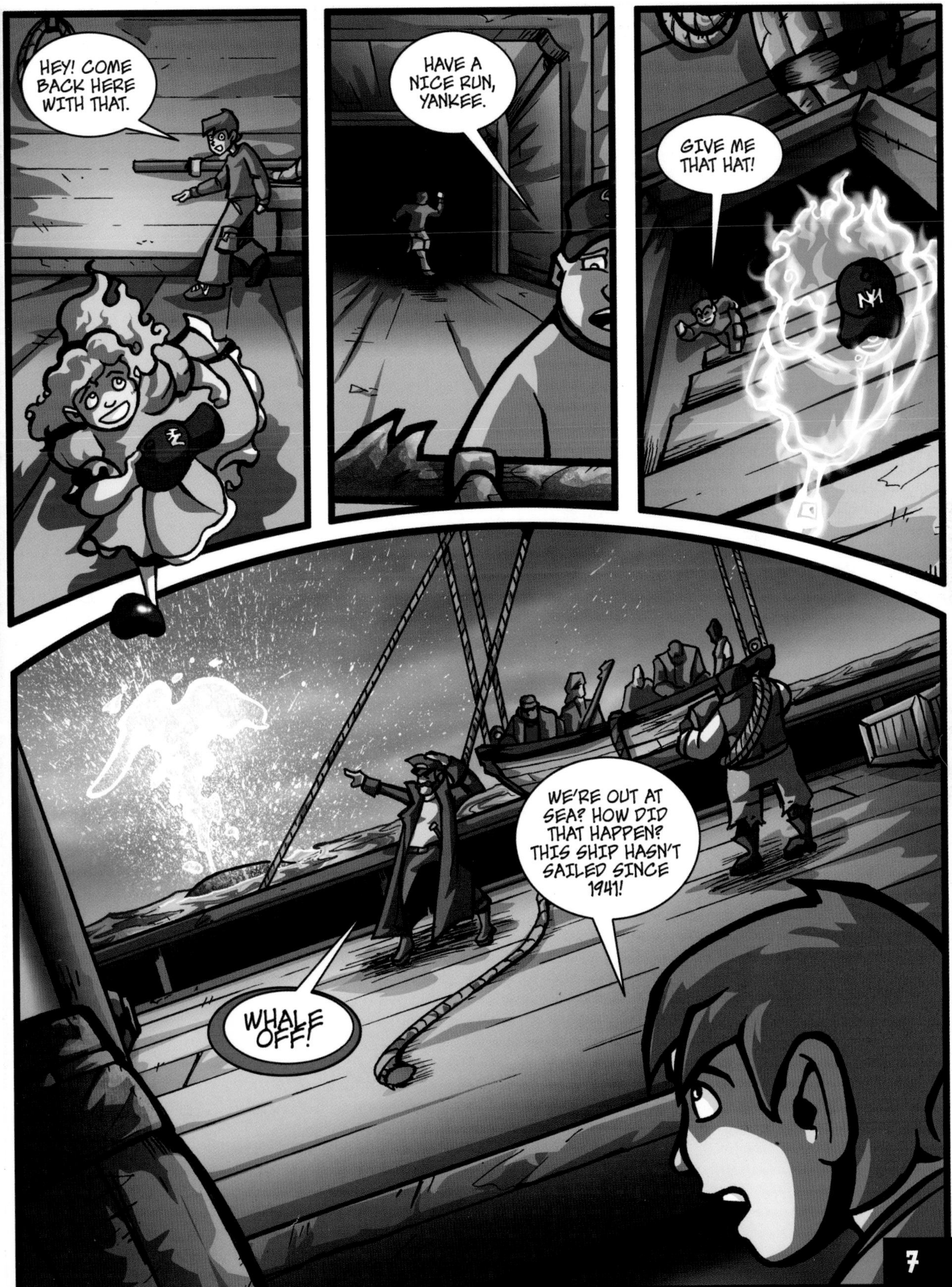
HEY! COME BACK HERE WITH THAT.
HAVE A NICE RUN, YANKEE.
GIVE ME THAT HAT!
WE'RE OUT AT SEA? HOW DID THAT HAPPEN? THIS SHIP HASN'T SAILED SINCE 1941!
WHALE OFF!

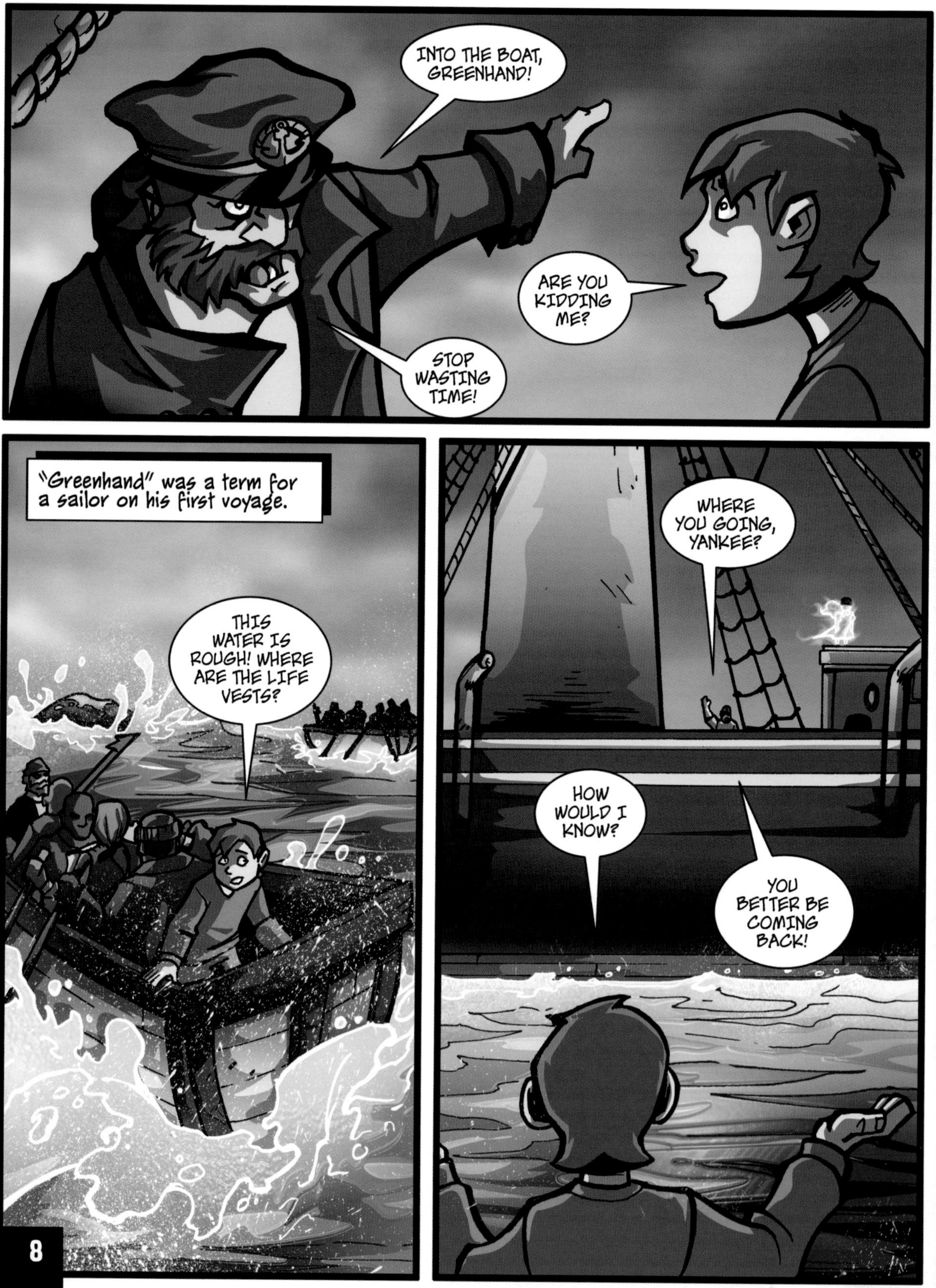
INTO THE BOAT, GREENHAND!
ARE YOU KIDDING ME?
STOP WASTING TIME!
"Greenhand" was a term for a sailor on his first voyage.
THIS WATER IS ROUGH! WHERE ARE THE LIFE VESTS?
WHERE YOU GOING, YANKEE?
HOW WOULD I KNOW?
YOU BETTER BE COMING BACK!

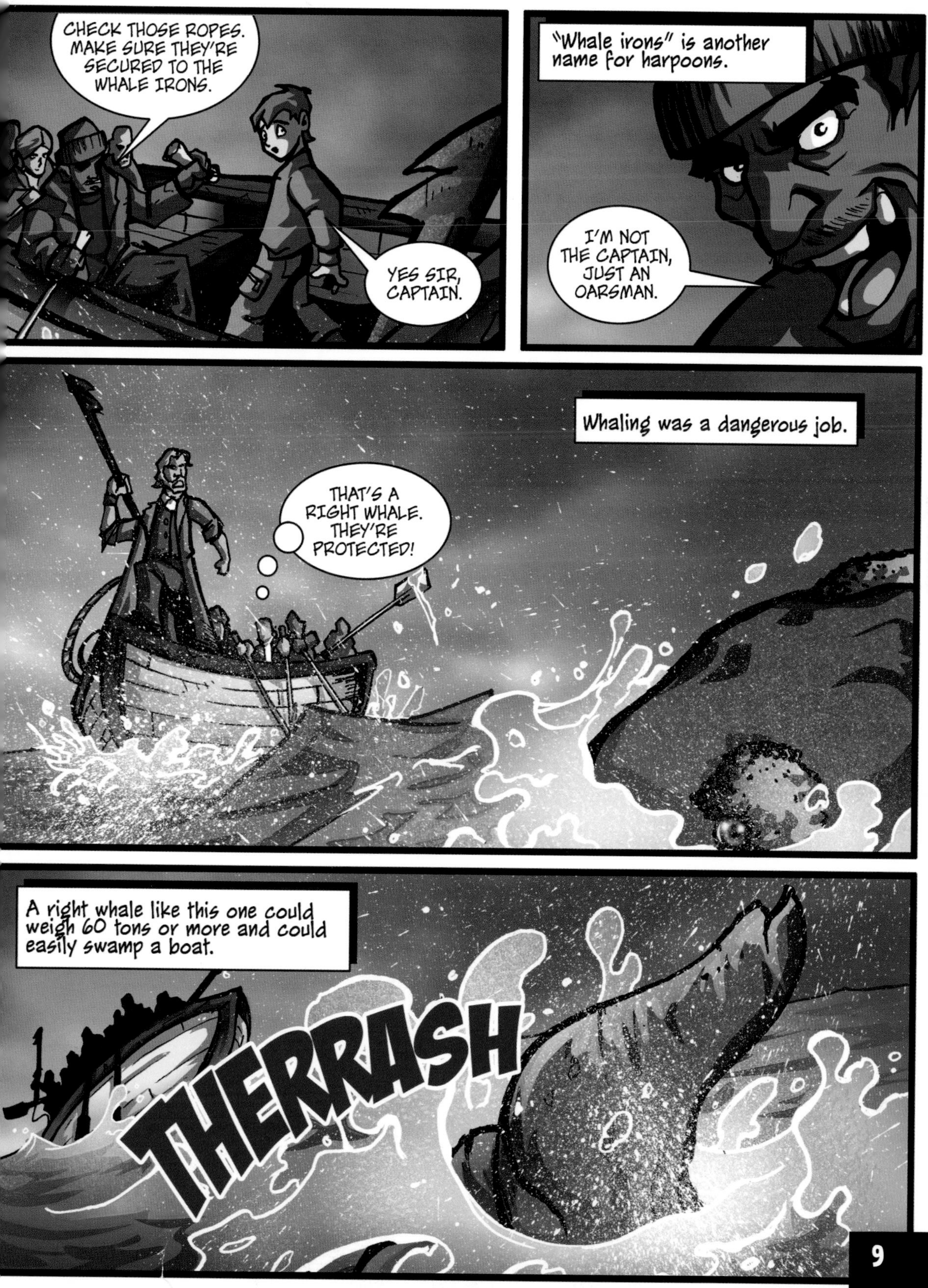
CHECK THOSE ROPES. MAKE SURE THEY'RE SECURED TO THE WHALE IRONS.
YES SIR, CAPTAIN.
"Whale irons" is another name for harpoons.
I'M NOT THE CAPTAIN, JUST AN OARSMAN.
Whaling was a dangerous job.
THAT'S A RIGHT WHALE. THEY'RE PROTECTED!
A right whale like this one could weigh 60 tons or more and could easily swamp a boat.
THERRASH

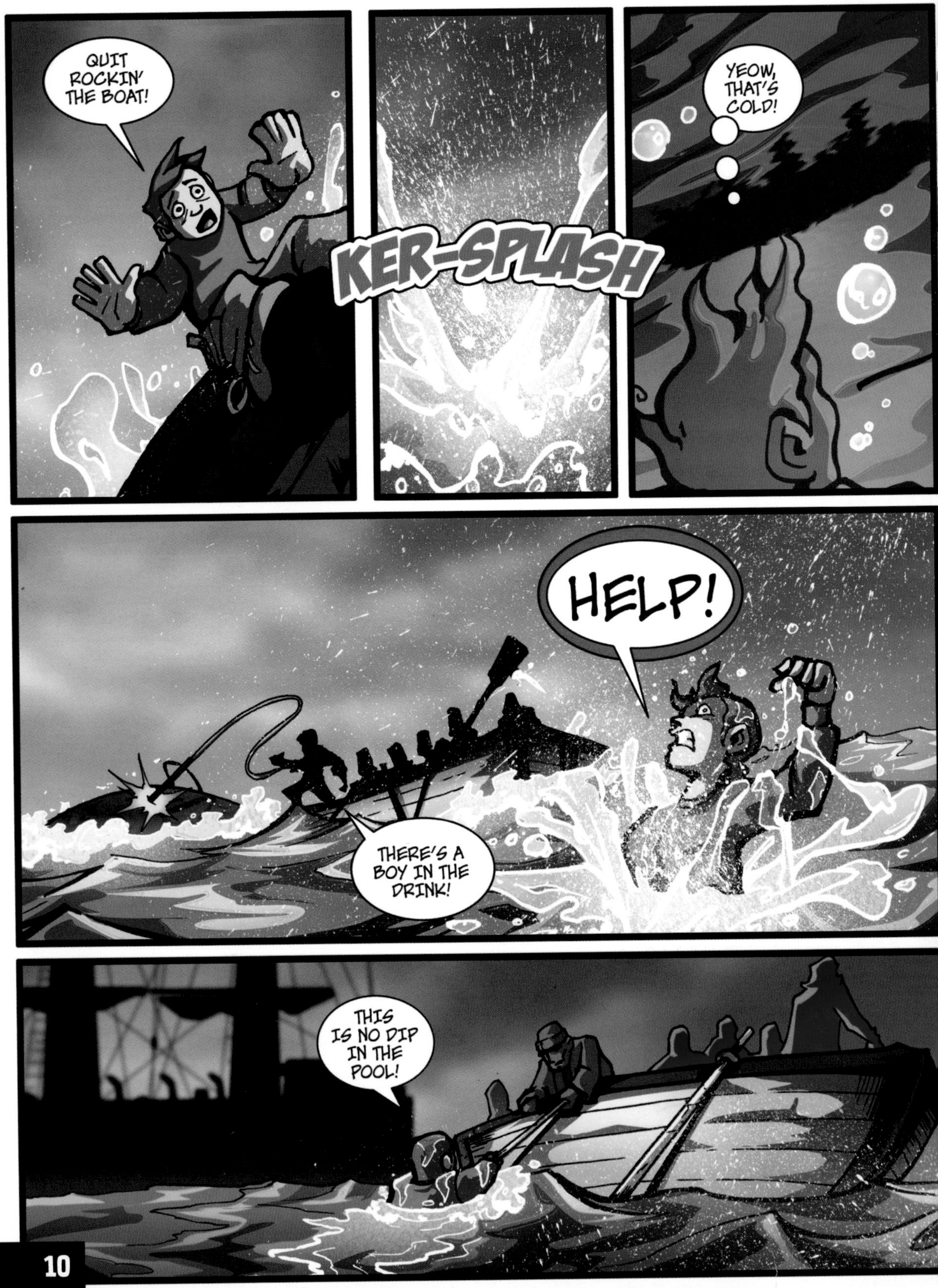
QUIT ROCKIN' THE BOAT!
KER-SPLASH
YEOW, THAT'S COLD!
HELP!
THERE'S A BOY IN THE DRINK!
THIS IS NO DIP IN THE POOL!

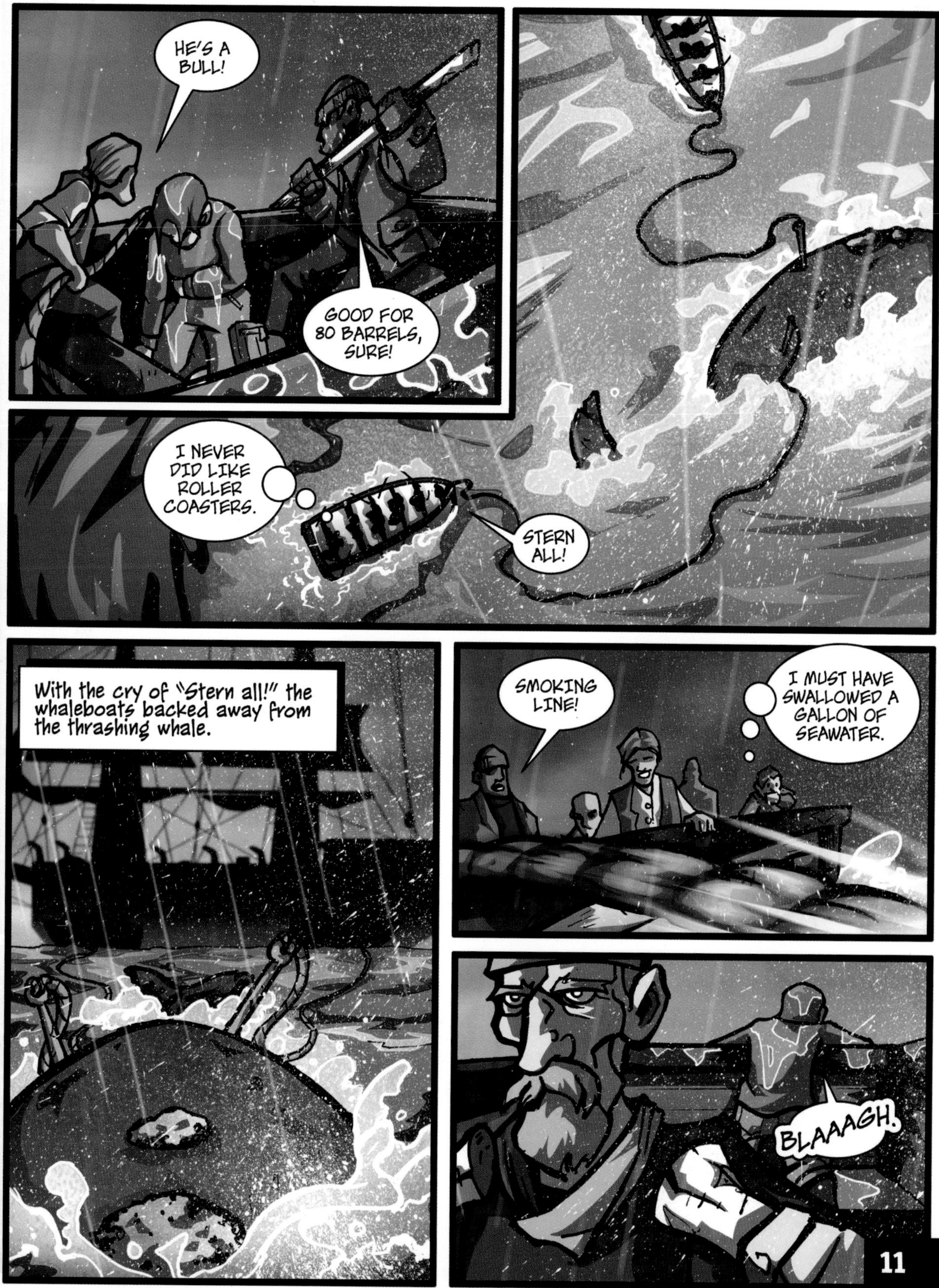
HE'S A BULL!
GOOD FOR 80 BARRELS, SURE!
I NEVER DID LIKE ROLLER COASTERS.
STERN ALL!
With the cry of "Stern all!" the whaleboats backed away from the thrashing whale.
SMOKING LINE!
I MUST HAVE SWALLOWED A GALLON OF SEAWATER.
BLAAAGH!

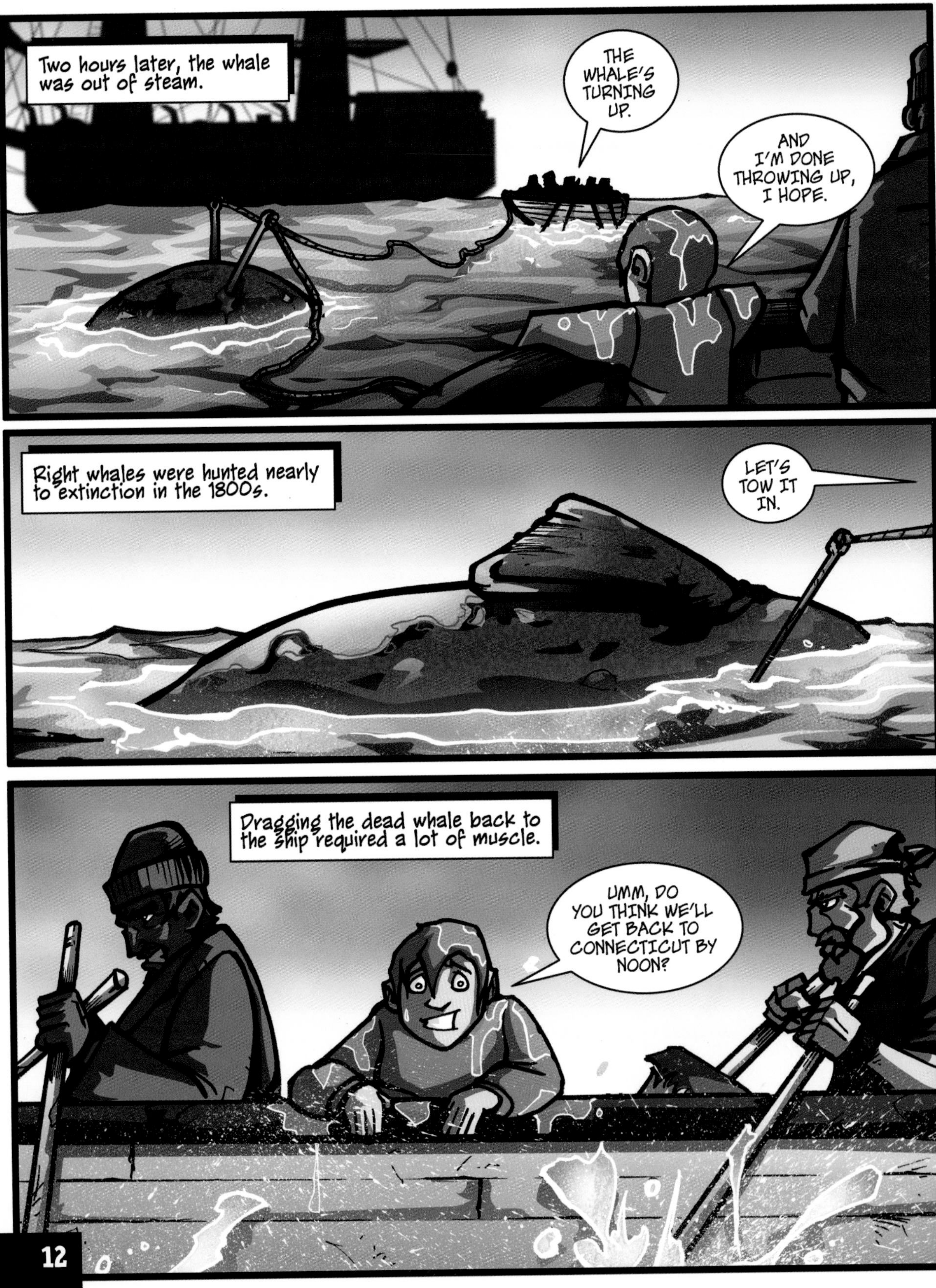
Two hours later, the whale was out of steam.
THE WHALE'S TURNING UP.
AND I'M DONE THROWING UP, I HOPE.
Right whales were hunted nearly to extinction in the 1800s.
LET'S TOW IT IN.
Dragging the dead whale back to the ship required a lot of muscle.
UMM, DO YOU THINK WE'LL GET BACK TO CONNECTICUT BY NOON?

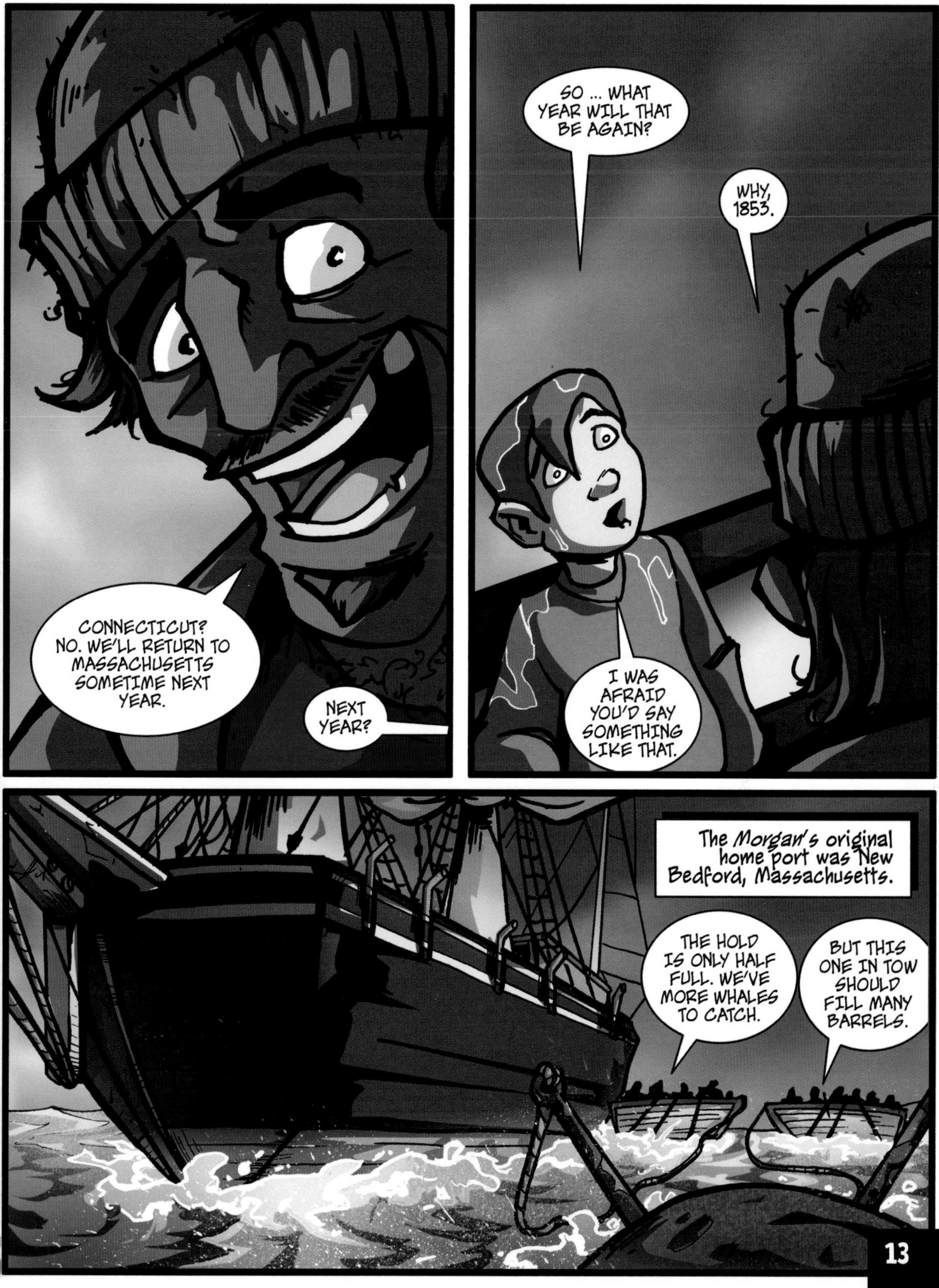
CONNECTICUT? NO. WE'LL RETURN TO MASSACHUSETTS SOMETIME NEXT YEAR.
NEXT YEAR?
SO ... WHAT YEAR WILL THAT BE AGAIN?
WHY, 1853.
I WAS AFRAID YOU'D SAY SOMETHING LIKE THAT.
The *Morgan's* original home port was New Bedford, Massachusetts.
THE HOLD IS ONLY HALF FULL. WE'VE MORE WHALES TO CATCH.
BUT THIS ONE IN TOW SHOULD FILL MANY BARRELS.

The crew secured the whale to the starboard side of the ship with heavy chains. Then the blubber was stripped off and its precious oil was processed.

YOU CAUGHT ONE!

IT NEARLY KILLED US. I WAS UNDERWATER FOREVER!

LET'S FIND A PLACE TO HIDE WHILE THEY'RE DEALING WITH THAT CARCASS. I'VE DONE ENOUGH WORK FOR ONE DAY.

I FOUND THE SLEEPING QUARTERS WHILE YOU WERE CHASING THE WHALE. THEY'RE DOWN HERE.

Most of the crew slept in the forecastle, a cramped, dark, dingy space under the main deck.

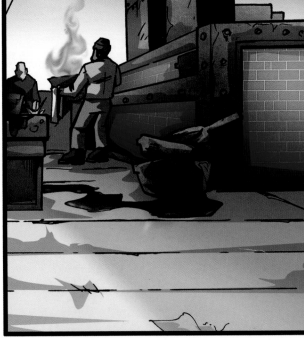

The strips of blubber were cut into "blanket pieces," which could weigh as much as a ton. Those pieces were divided into "horse pieces," and finally into smaller "Bible pieces," which went into the trypots.

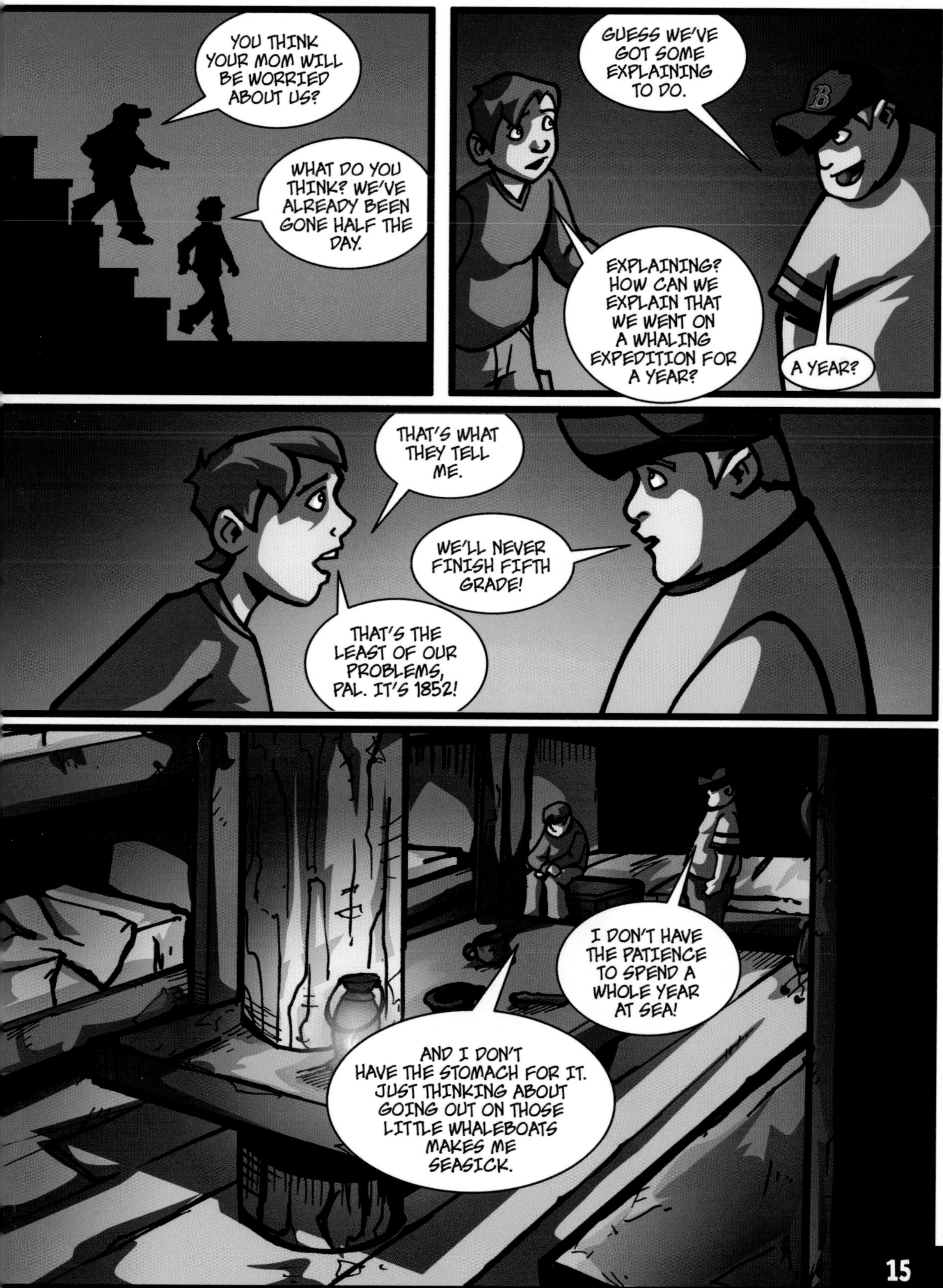
YOU THINK YOUR MOM WILL BE WORRIED ABOUT US?
WHAT DO YOU THINK? WE'VE ALREADY BEEN GONE HALF THE DAY.
GUESS WE'VE GOT SOME EXPLAINING TO DO.
EXPLAINING? HOW CAN WE EXPLAIN THAT WE WENT ON A WHALING EXPEDITION FOR A YEAR?
A YEAR?
THAT'S WHAT THEY TELL ME.
WE'LL NEVER FINISH FIFTH GRADE!
THAT'S THE LEAST OF OUR PROBLEMS, PAL. IT'S 1852!
I DON'T HAVE THE PATIENCE TO SPEND A WHOLE YEAR AT SEA!
AND I DON'T HAVE THE STOMACH FOR IT. JUST THINKING ABOUT GOING OUT ON THOSE LITTLE WHALEBOATS MAKES ME SEASICK.

Fleas, cockroaches, and bedbugs were constant companions on a whaling ship.

SO HOW DO WE GET OUT OF THIS MESS?

I DON'T KNOW YET.

THWACK

IT SURE IS HOT DOWN HERE.

YEAH, AND IT SMELLS LIKE ROTTEN BLUBBER.

WISH WE COULD SNEAK UPSTAIRS AND GET SOME AIR.

THAT'S IT!

WHAT'S IT?

THE CAP.

YOU WANT TO WEAR IT?

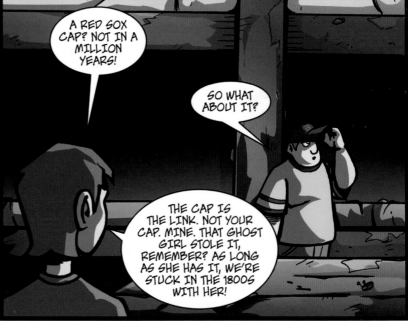

A RED SOX CAP? NOT IN A MILLION YEARS!

SO WHAT ABOUT IT?

THE CAP IS THE LINK. NOT YOUR CAP. MINE. THAT GHOST GIRL STOLE IT, REMEMBER? AS LONG AS SHE HAS IT, WE'RE STUCK IN THE 1800S WITH HER!

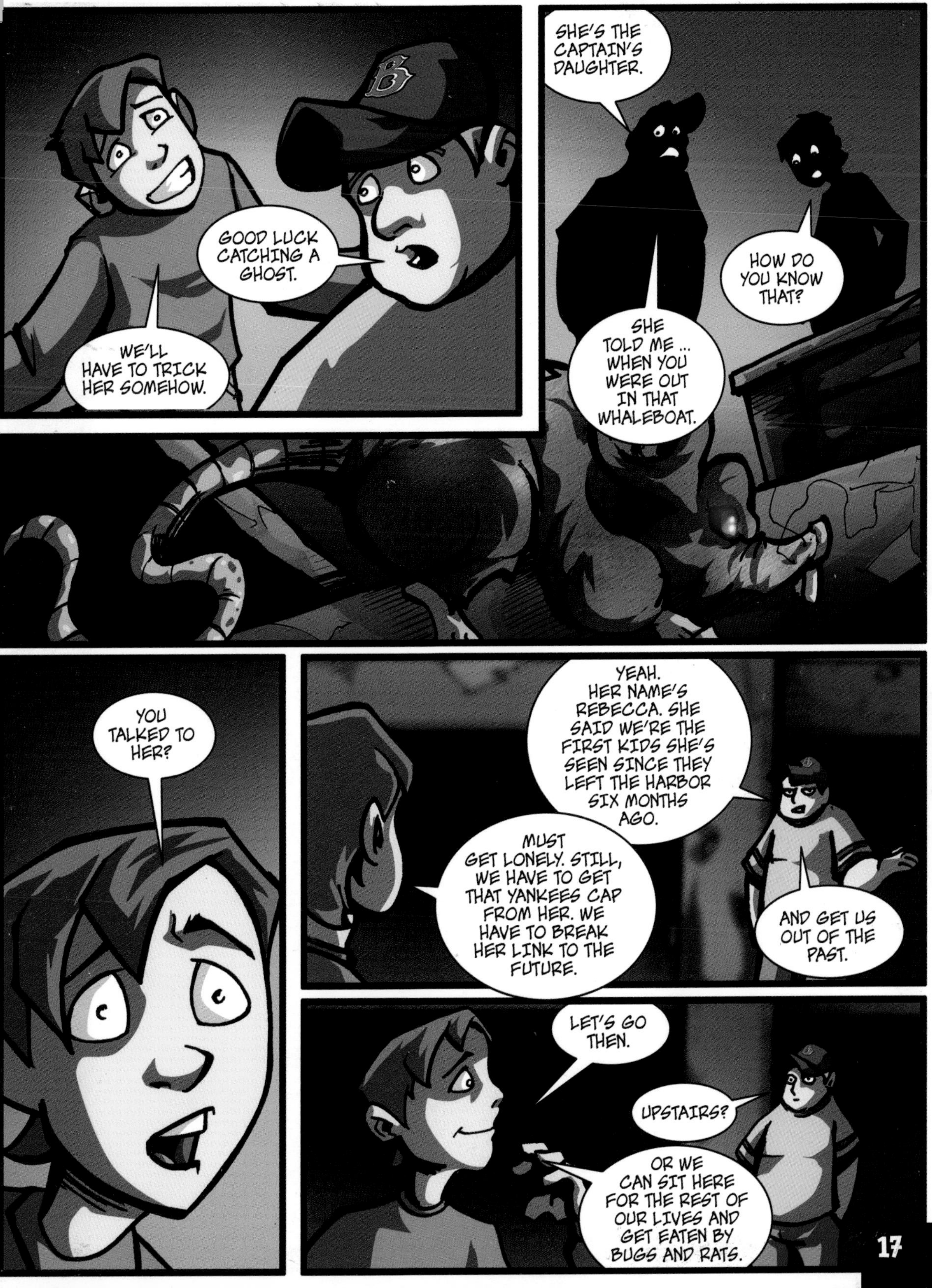
GOOD LUCK CATCHING A GHOST.
WE'LL HAVE TO TRICK HER SOMEHOW.
SHE'S THE CAPTAIN'S DAUGHTER.
HOW DO YOU KNOW THAT?
SHE TOLD ME ... WHEN YOU WERE OUT IN THAT WHALEBOAT.
YOU TALKED TO HER?
YEAH. HER NAME'S REBECCA. SHE SAID WE'RE THE FIRST KIDS SHE'S SEEN SINCE THEY LEFT THE HARBOR SIX MONTHS AGO.
MUST GET LONELY. STILL, WE HAVE TO GET THAT YANKEES CAP FROM HER. WE HAVE TO BREAK HER LINK TO THE FUTURE.
AND GET US OUT OF THE PAST.
LET'S GO THEN.
UPSTAIRS?
OR WE CAN SIT HERE FOR THE REST OF OUR LIVES AND GET EATEN BY BUGS AND RATS.

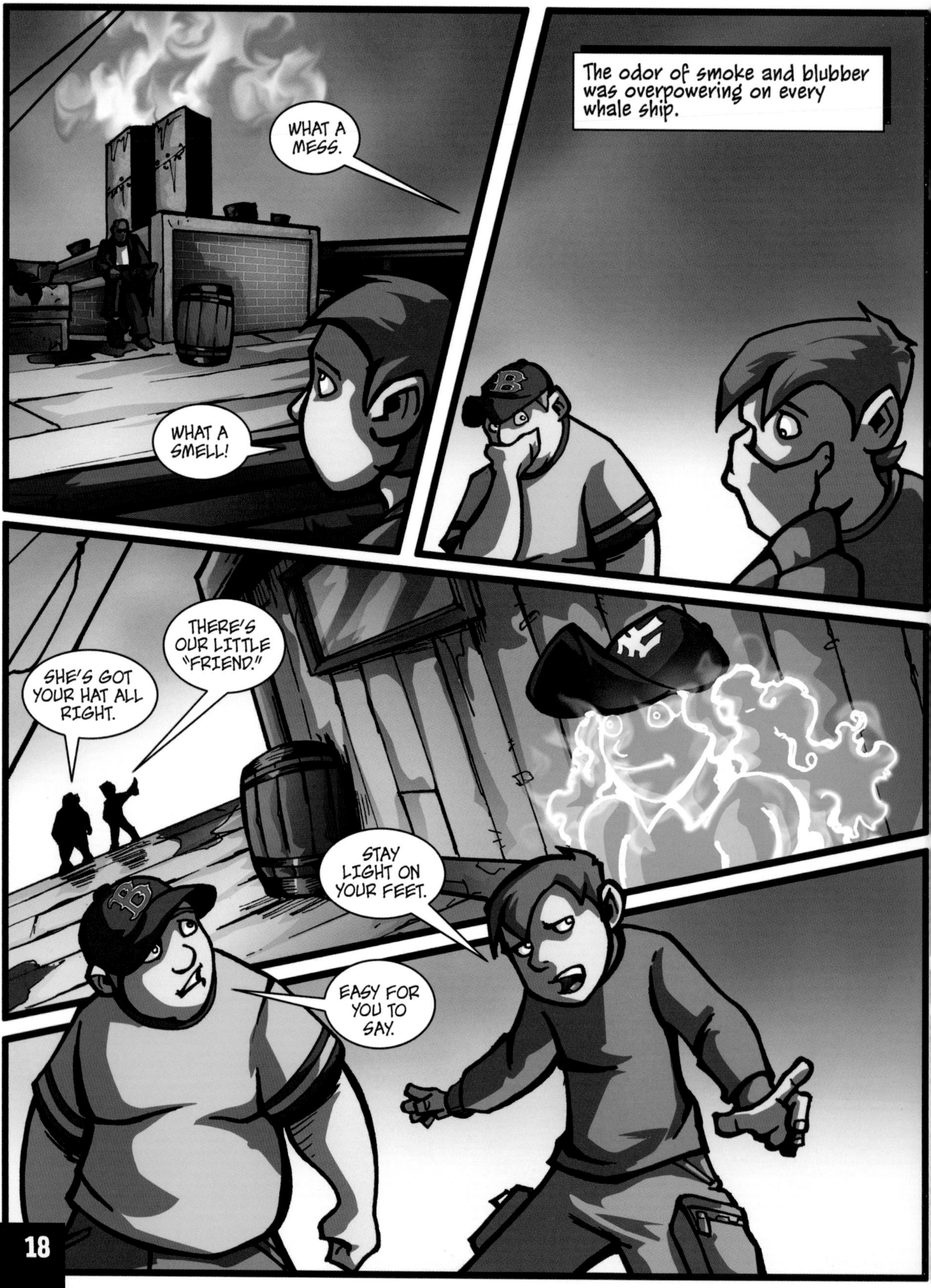
WHAT A MESS.
WHAT A SMELL!
The odor of smoke and blubber was overpowering on every whale ship.
THERE'S OUR LITTLE "FRIEND."
SHE'S GOT YOUR HAT ALL RIGHT.
STAY LIGHT ON YOUR FEET.
EASY FOR YOU TO SAY.

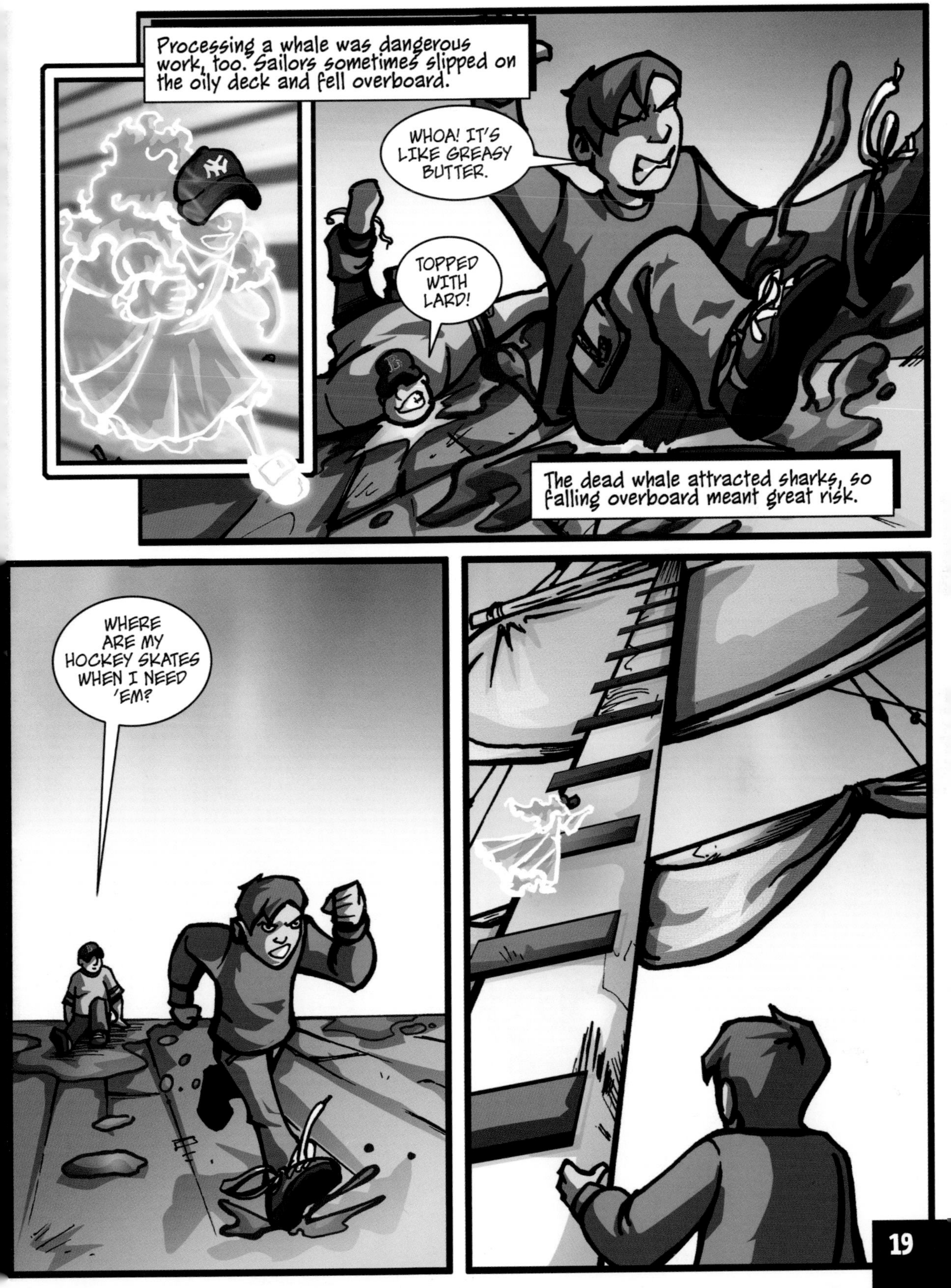
Processing a whale was dangerous work, too. Sailors sometimes slipped on the oily deck and fell overboard.
WHOA! IT'S LIKE GREASY BUTTER.
TOPPED WITH LARD!
The dead whale attracted sharks, so falling overboard meant great risk.
WHERE ARE MY HOCKEY SKATES WHEN I NEED 'EM?

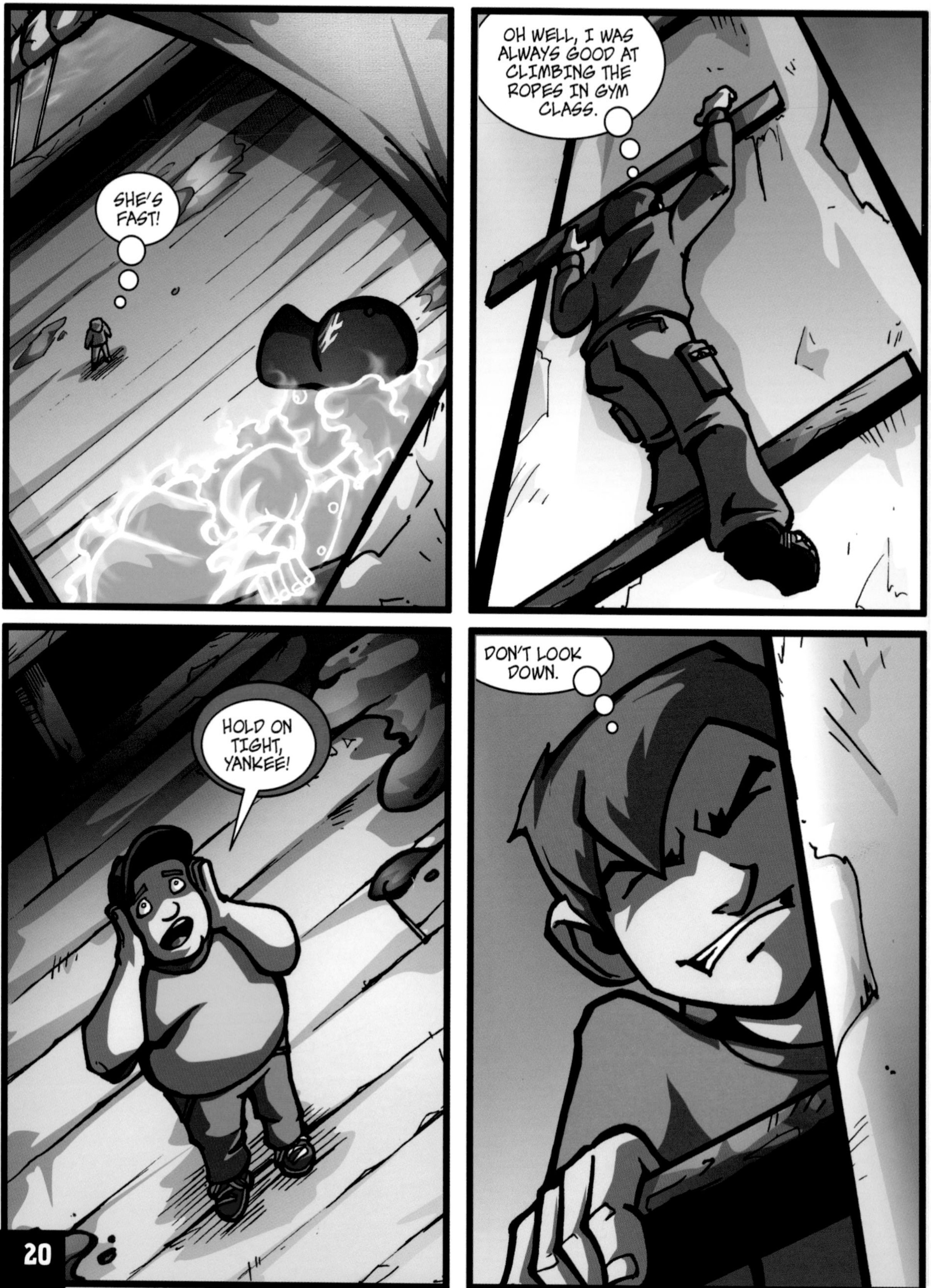
SHE'S FAST!
OH WELL, I WAS ALWAYS GOOD AT CLIMBING THE ROPES IN GYM CLASS.
HOLD ON TIGHT, YANKEE!
DON'T LOOK DOWN.

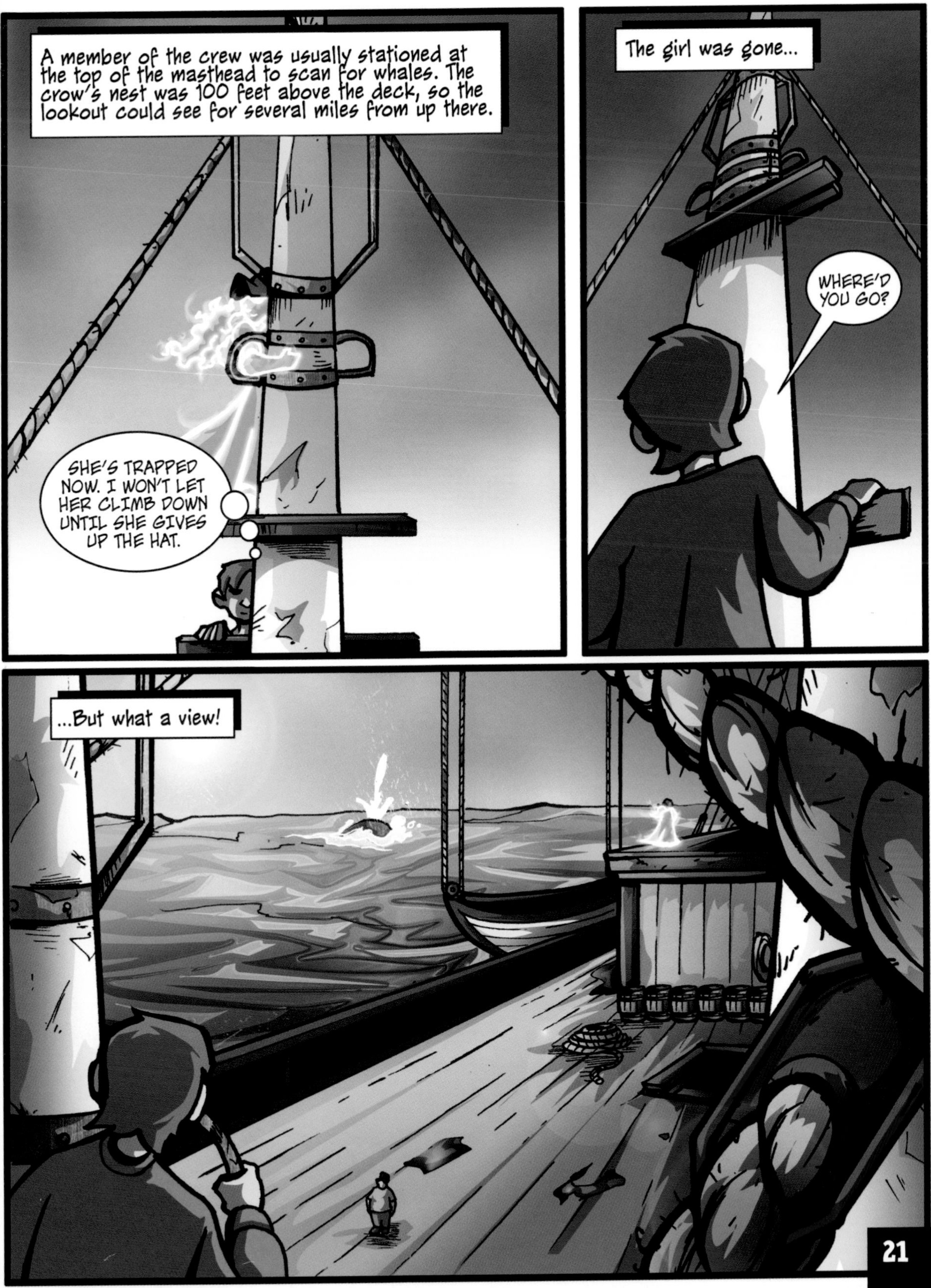
A member of the crew was usually stationed at the top of the masthead to scan for whales. The crow's nest was 100 feet above the deck, so the lookout could see for several miles from up there.
SHE'S TRAPPED NOW. I WON'T LET HER CLIMB DOWN UNTIL SHE GIVES UP THE HAT.
The girl was gone...
WHERE'D YOU GO?
...But what a view!

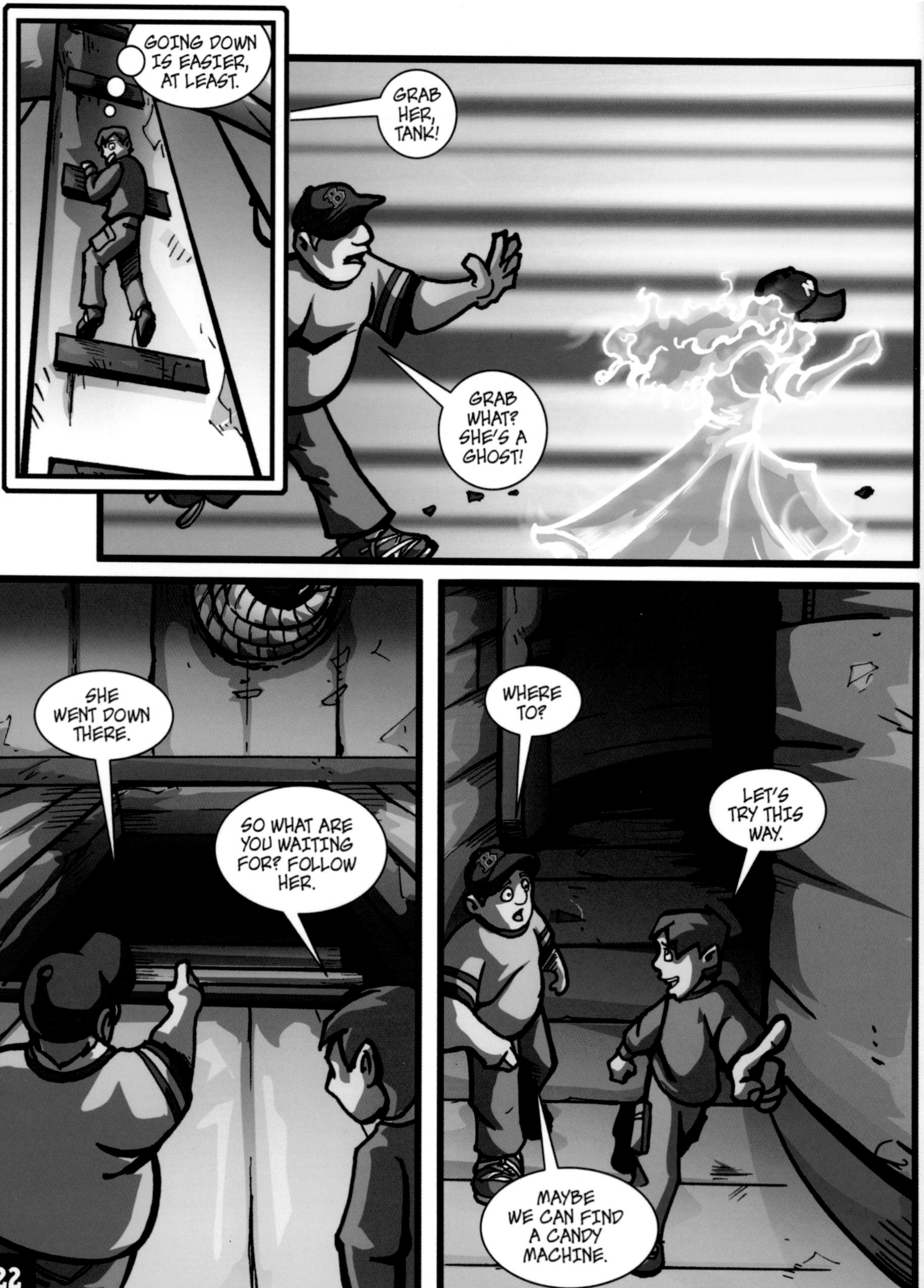
GOING DOWN IS EASIER, AT LEAST.
GRAB HER, TANK!
GRAB WHAT? SHE'S A GHOST!
SHE WENT DOWN THERE.
SO WHAT ARE YOU WAITING FOR? FOLLOW HER.
WHERE TO?
LET'S TRY THIS WAY.
MAYBE WE CAN FIND A CANDY MACHINE.

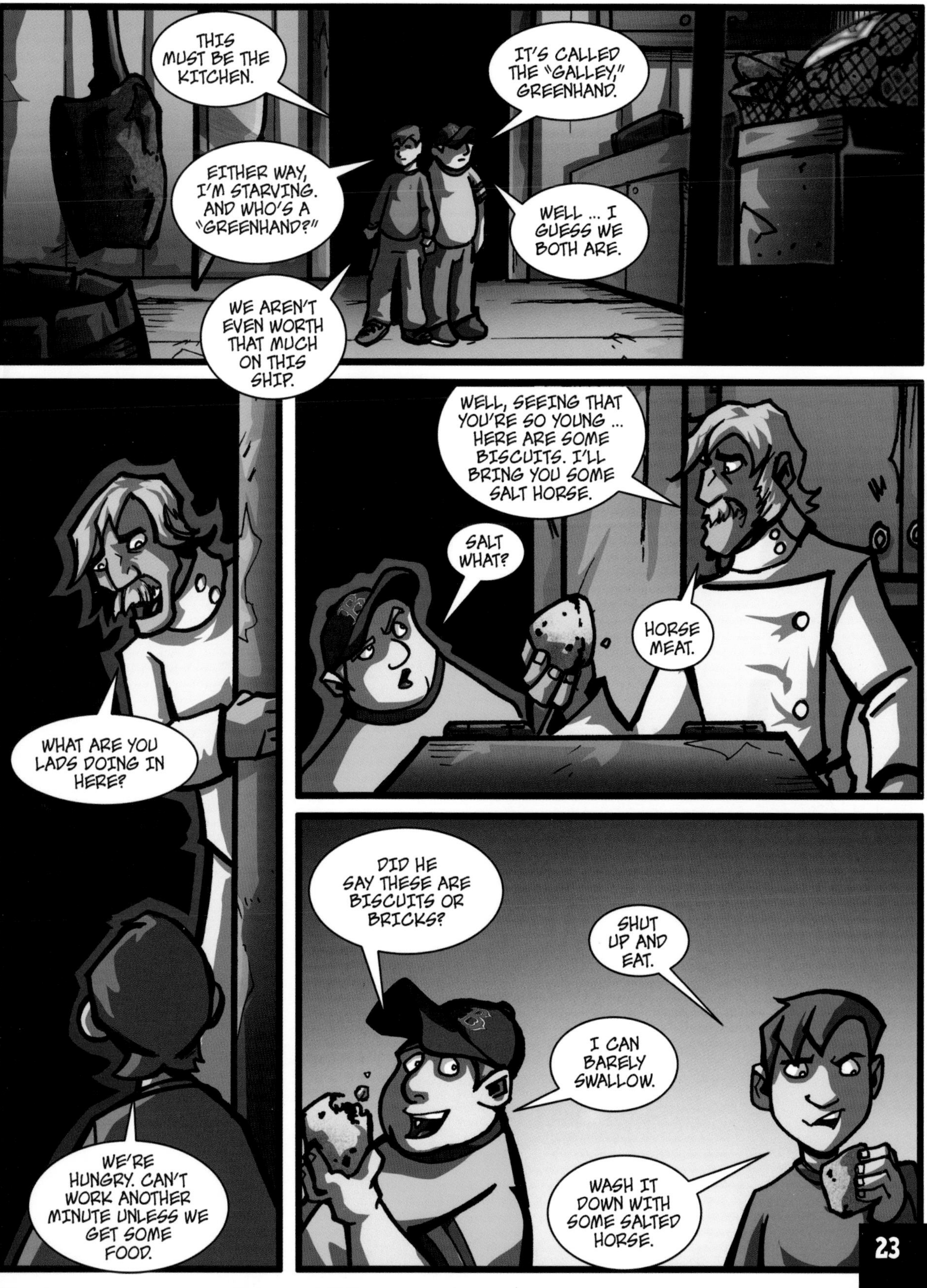
THIS MUST BE THE KITCHEN.
IT'S CALLED THE "GALLEY," GREENHAND.
EITHER WAY, I'M STARVING. AND WHO'S A "GREENHAND?"
WELL ... I GUESS WE BOTH ARE.
WE AREN'T EVEN WORTH THAT MUCH ON THIS SHIP.
WHAT ARE YOU LADS DOING IN HERE?
WE'RE HUNGRY. CAN'T WORK ANOTHER MINUTE UNLESS WE GET SOME FOOD.
WELL, SEEING THAT YOU'RE SO YOUNG ... HERE ARE SOME BISCUITS. I'LL BRING YOU SOME SALT HORSE.
SALT WHAT?
HORSE MEAT.
DID HE SAY THESE ARE BISCUITS OR BRICKS?
SHUT UP AND EAT.
I CAN BARELY SWALLOW.
WASH IT DOWN WITH SOME SALTED HORSE.

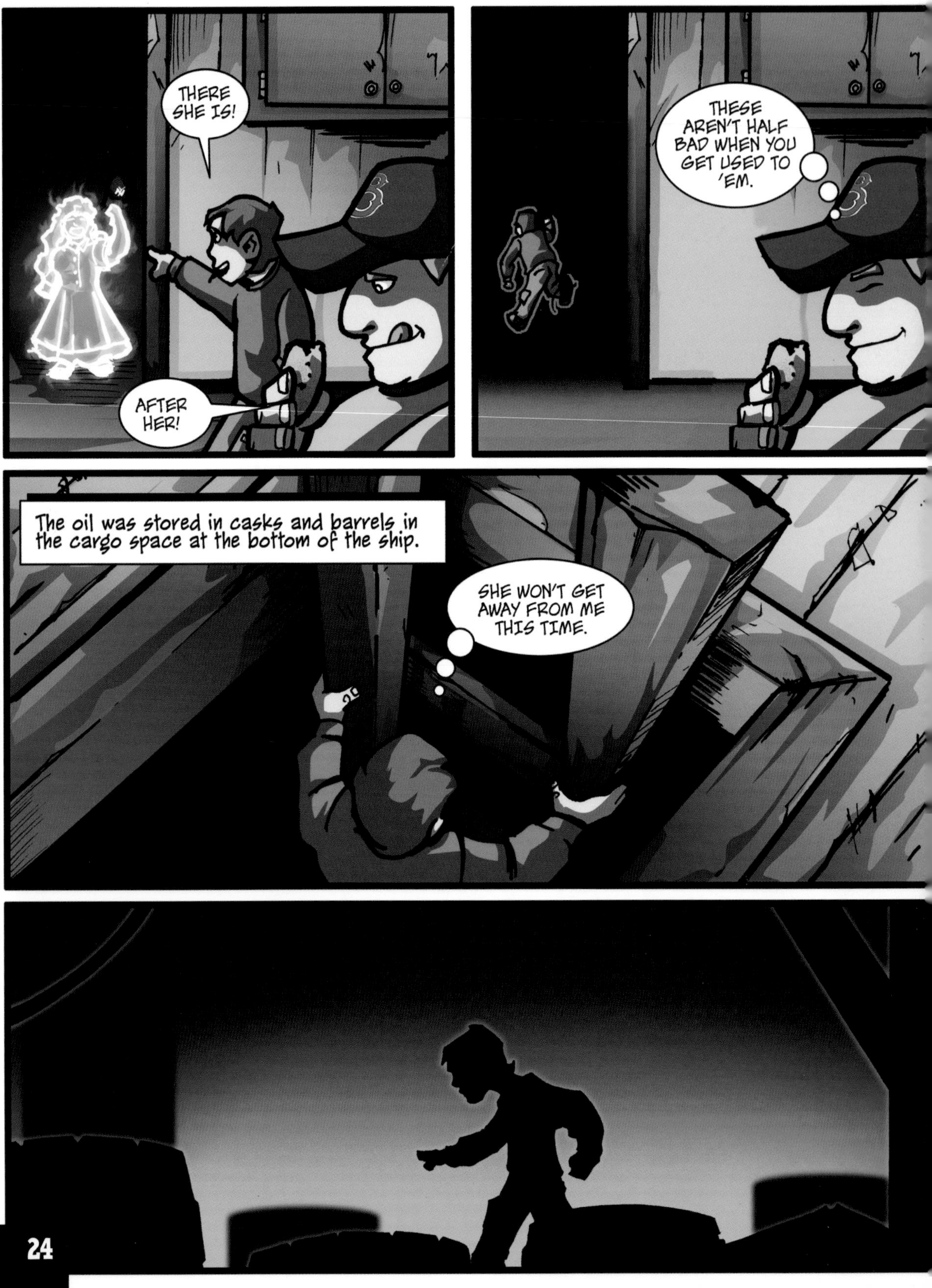
THERE SHE IS!
AFTER HER!
THESE AREN'T HALF BAD WHEN YOU GET USED TO 'EM.
The oil was stored in casks and barrels in the cargo space at the bottom of the ship.
SHE WON'T GET AWAY FROM ME THIS TIME.

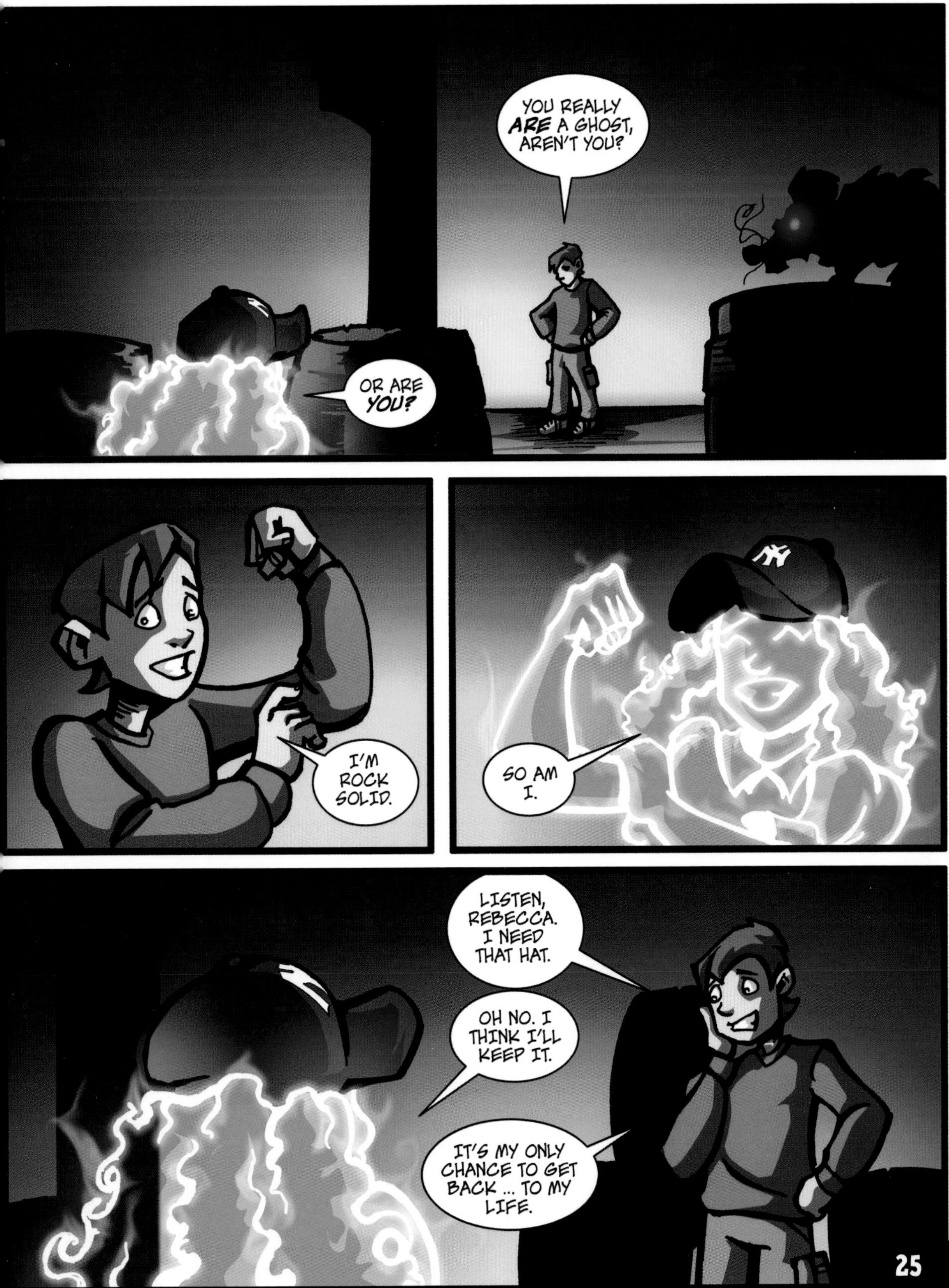
YOU REALLY ARE A GHOST, AREN'T YOU?
OR ARE YOU?
I'M ROCK SOLID.
SO AM I.
LISTEN, REBECCA. I NEED THAT HAT.
OH NO. I THINK I'LL KEEP IT.
IT'S MY ONLY CHANCE TO GET BACK ... TO MY LIFE.

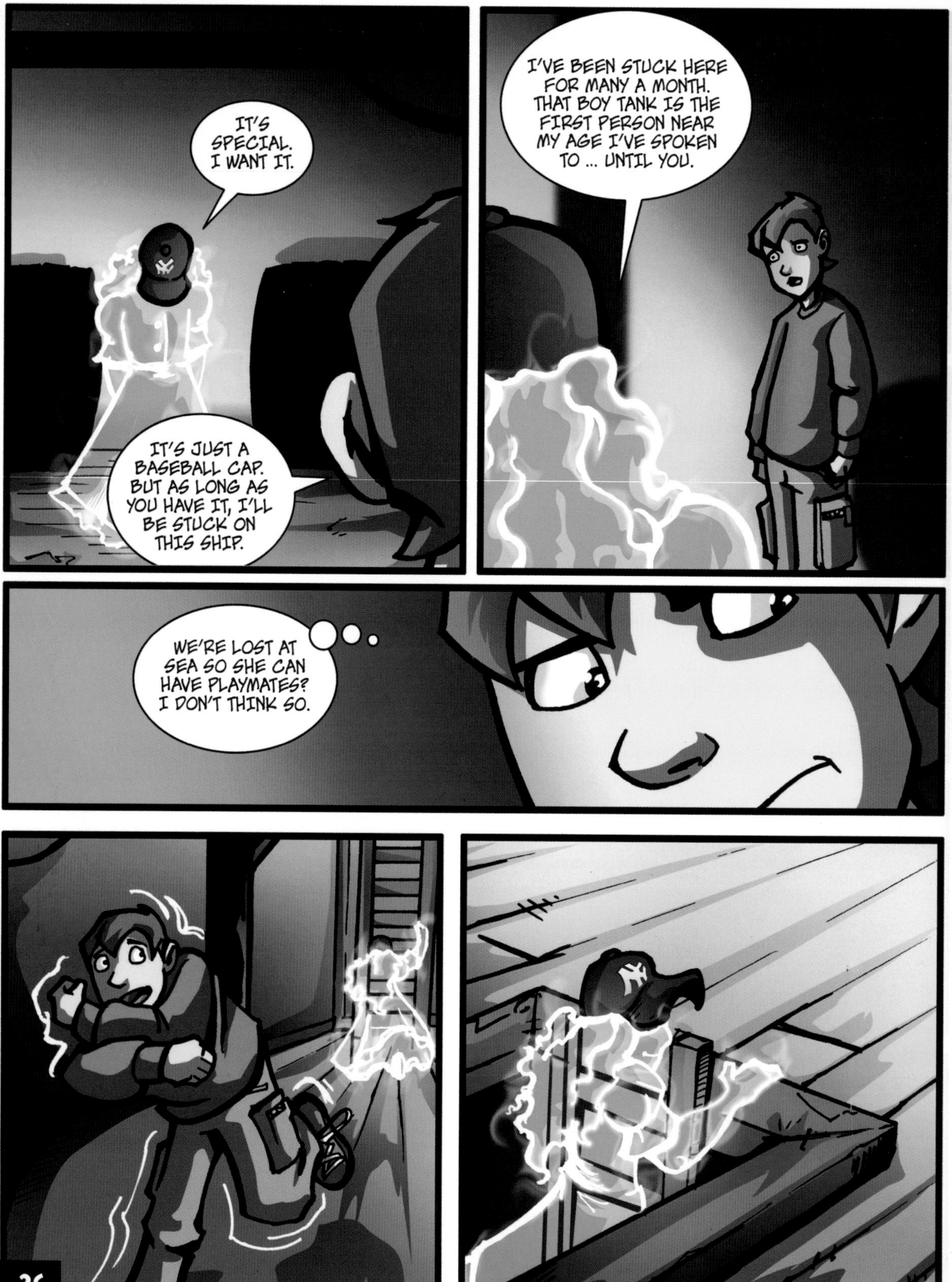
IT'S SPECIAL. I WANT IT.
IT'S JUST A BASEBALL CAP. BUT AS LONG AS YOU HAVE IT, I'LL BE STUCK ON THIS SHIP.
I'VE BEEN STUCK HERE FOR MANY A MONTH. THAT BOY TANK IS THE FIRST PERSON NEAR MY AGE I'VE SPOKEN TO ... UNTIL YOU.
WE'RE LOST AT SEA SO SHE CAN HAVE PLAYMATES? I DON'T THINK SO.

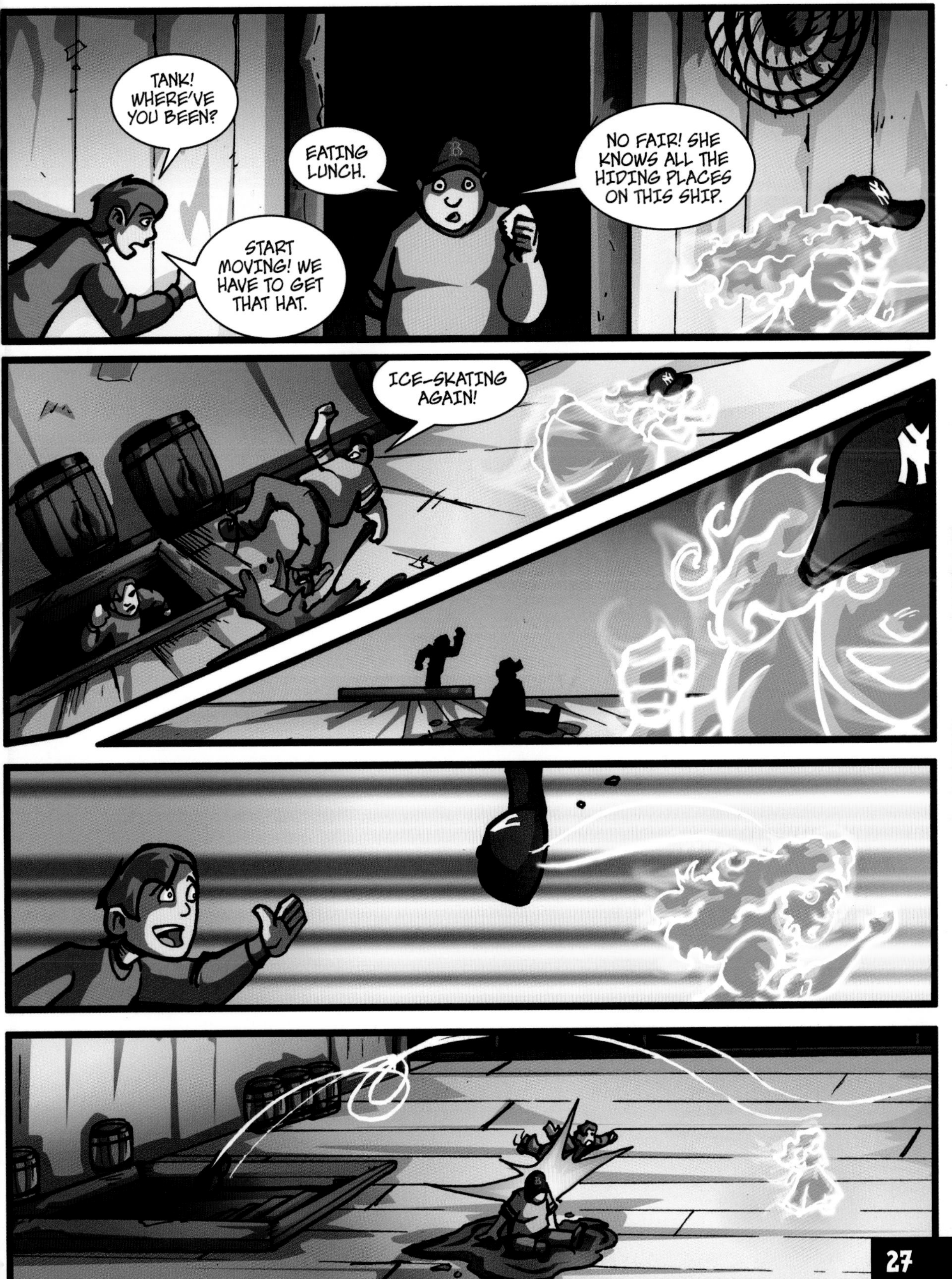
TANK! WHERE'VE YOU BEEN?
EATING LUNCH.
START MOVING! WE HAVE TO GET THAT HAT.
NO FAIR! SHE KNOWS ALL THE HIDING PLACES ON THIS SHIP.
ICE-SKATING AGAIN!

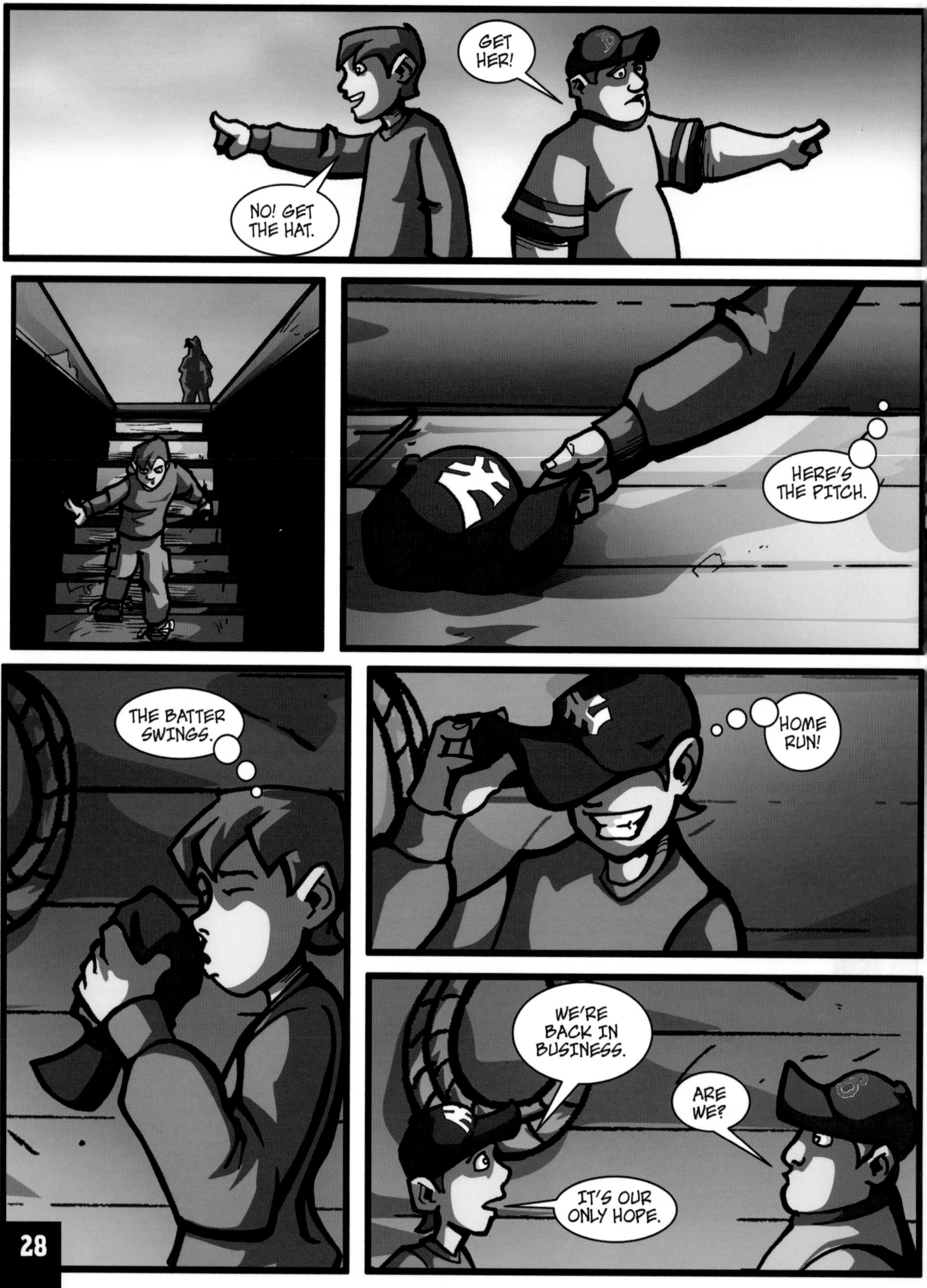
GET HER!
NO! GET THE HAT.
HERE'S THE PITCH.
THE BATTER SWINGS.
HOME RUN!
WE'RE BACK IN BUSINESS.
ARE WE?
IT'S OUR ONLY HOPE.

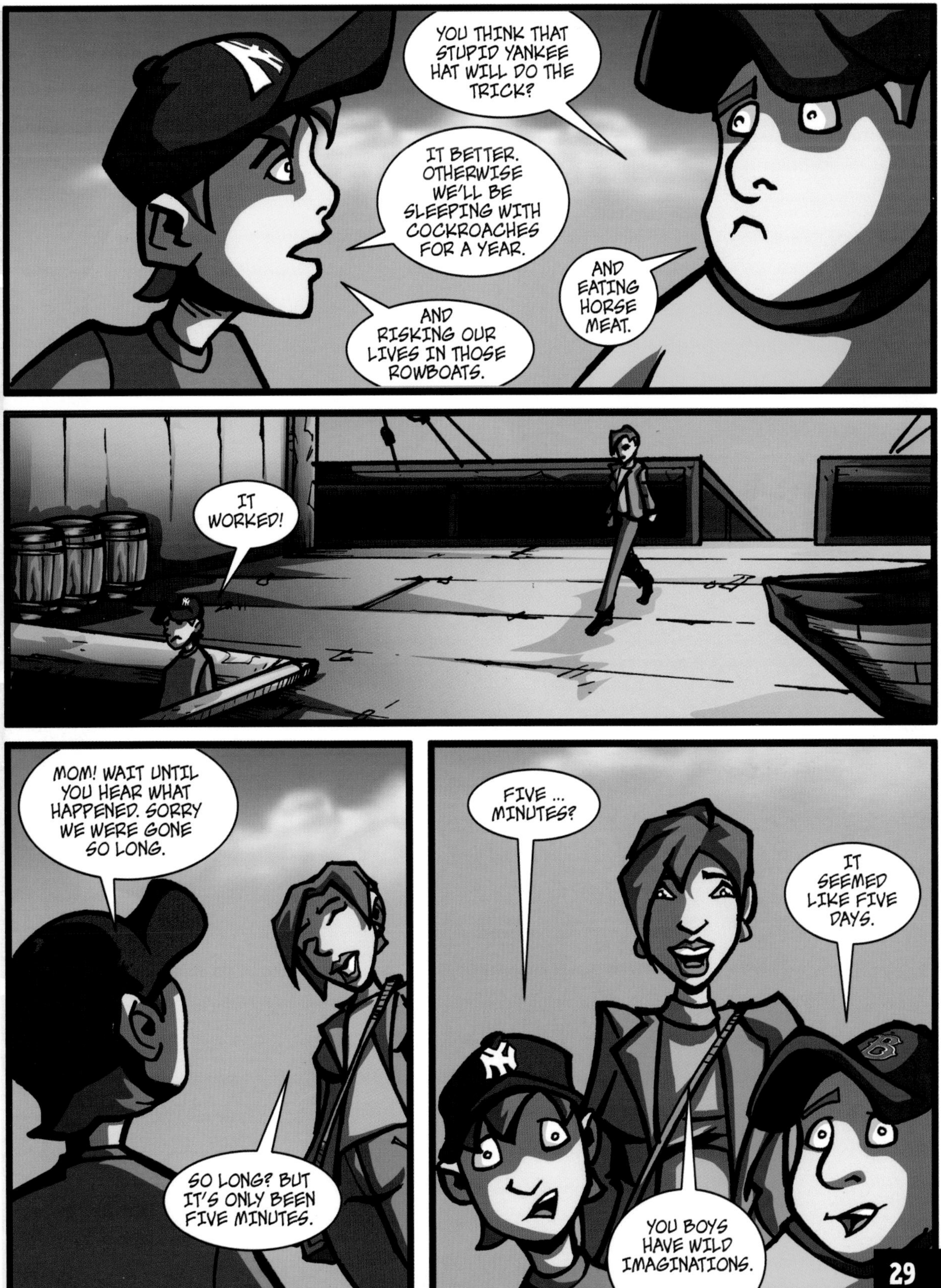
YOU THINK THAT STUPID YANKEE HAT WILL DO THE TRICK?
IT BETTER. OTHERWISE WE'LL BE SLEEPING WITH COCKROACHES FOR A YEAR.
AND EATING HORSE MEAT.
AND RISKING OUR LIVES IN THOSE ROWBOATS.
IT WORKED!
MOM! WAIT UNTIL YOU HEAR WHAT HAPPENED. SORRY WE WERE GONE SO LONG.
SO LONG? BUT IT'S ONLY BEEN FIVE MINUTES.
FIVE ... MINUTES?
IT SEEMED LIKE FIVE DAYS.
YOU BOYS HAVE WILD IMAGINATIONS.

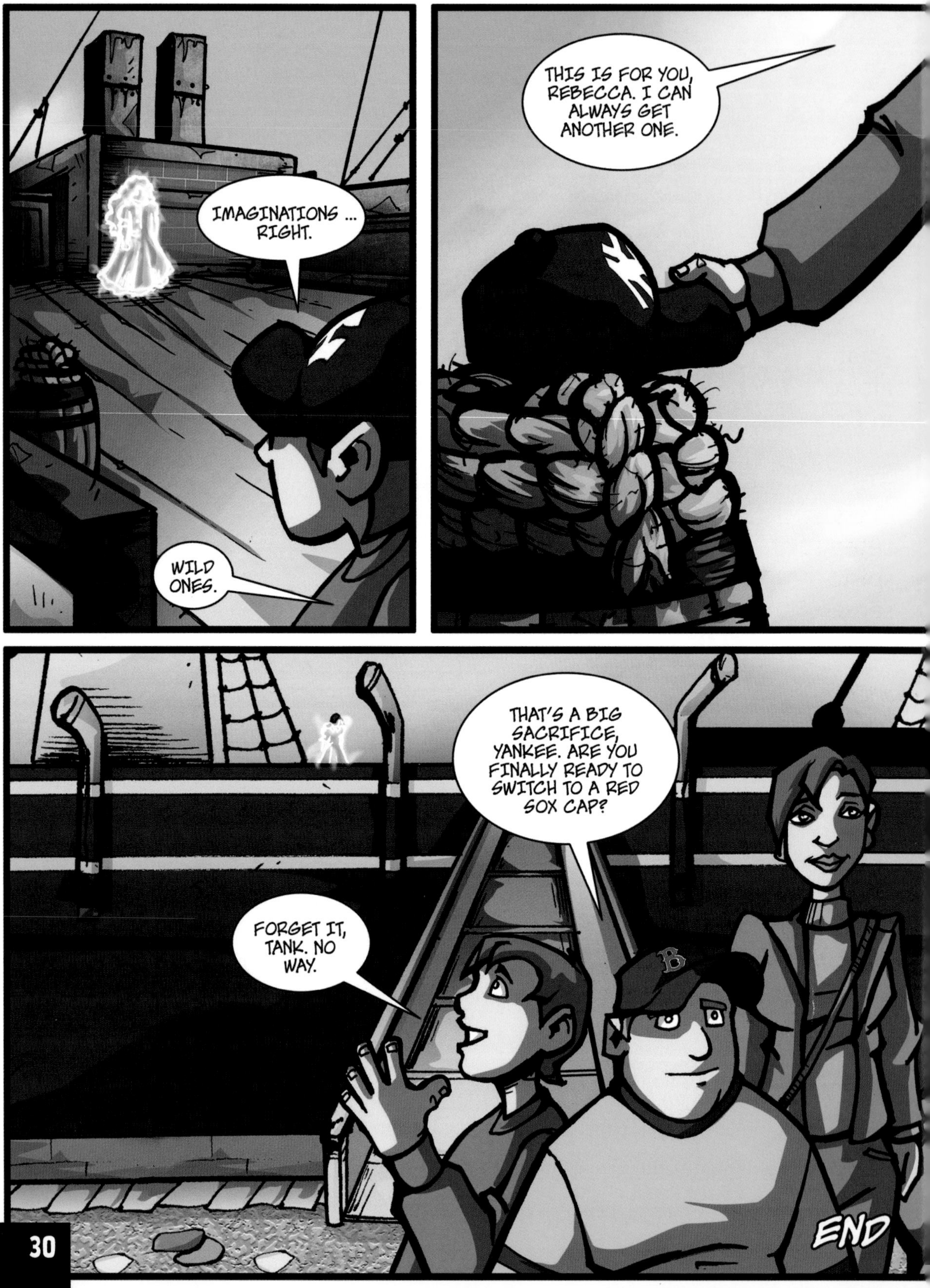
IMAGINATIONS ... RIGHT.
WILD ONES.
THIS IS FOR YOU, REBECCA. I CAN ALWAYS GET ANOTHER ONE.
THAT'S A BIG SACRIFICE, YANKEE. ARE YOU FINALLY READY TO SWITCH TO A RED SOX CAP?
FORGET IT, TANK. NO WAY.
END

THE *CHARLES W. MORGAN*

About 1,000 sailors worked on the *Charles W. Morgan* at one time or another during its 80 years of service. Many people believe that some of those sailors still reside on the ship—as ghosts.

The *Charles W. Morgan* is the only ninteenth-century wooden whaling ship still in existence. It is a National Historic Landmark. It's also one of the main attractions at the Mystic Seaport maritime museum in Connecticut.

Over the years, the ship's visitors have reported seeing a ghost dressed in 1800s clothing sitting on a pile of rope. When a team of researchers spent a night onboard, they claimed to have detected the spirits of the ship's cook and a little girl. They also reported feeling a sense of "sickness and despair" among a ghostly group of fifteen sailors during a heavy storm at sea.

Between 1841 and 1921, the *Morgan* made 37 voyages throughout the world in search of whales. The journeys lasted from nine months to five years and were usually very successful. There were about 30 sailors aboard for each trip. Sometimes a captain would bring his wife and children along.

Some species of whales, such as the right whale, were hunted nearly to extinction in the 1800s. The League of Nations put right whales under protection from hunting in 1935. Today, right whale populations have finally begun to grow again.

GLOSSARY

blubber - a layer of fat in whales and other marine mammals. Blubber provides these animals with insulation, food storage, and padding.

harpoon - a long spear made from driftwood or whale bone used to kill seals, walrus, and whales.

home port - the port where a ship comes from.

oarsman - one who rows.

rivalry - being in competition.

smoking line - a term used for the line being pulled out by a diving whale. This crew let the line run out so the whale wouldn't pull the boat underwater with it. The line went out so fast it smoked.

starboard - the right side of a ship when looking forward.

stern - the rear of a ship.

tryworks - large rectangular boxes that held cauldrons over a fire that was separated from the ship by bricks and a pool of water. The pots melted the blubber into oil to be sold later.

whaling - the act, business, or work of hunting and killing whales for their oil, flesh, and bone.

WEB SITES

To learn more about the *Charles W. Morgan*, visit ABDO Group online at **www.abdopublishing.com**. Web sites about the ship are featured on our Book Links page. These links are routinely monitored and updated to provide the most current information available.